Dedicated with thanks to Chris Chapman,
who first introduced me to the writings of Etty Hillesum
AB

For Katie, Benny, George & Maggie
DL

Anne Booth was inspired to write this book by the words of Etty Hillesum,

a Jewish woman and victim of the Holocaust who wrote:

"Give your sorrow all the space and shelter in yourself that is its due,

for if everyone bears grief honestly and courageously, the sorrow that now fills the world will abate.

But if you do instead reserve most of the space inside you for hatred and thoughts of revenge –

from which new sorrows will be born for others – then sorrow will never cease in this world.

And if you have given sorrow the space it demands, then you may truly say: life is beautiful and so rich."

Esther 'Etty' Hillesum (15 Jan 1914 – 30 Nov 1943)

A TEMPLAR BOOK

This edition published in the UK in 2022 by Templar Books.
First published in the UK in 2021 by Templar Books,
an imprint of Bonnier Books UK,
4th Floor, Victoria House
Bloomsbury Square, London WC1B 4DA
Owned by Bonnier Books
Sveavägen 56, Stockholm, Sweden
www.bonnierbooks.co.uk

Text copyright © 2021 by Anne Booth
Illustrations copyright © 2021 David Litchfield

1 3 5 7 9 10 8 6 4 2

Paperback ISBN 978-1-80078-087-3
eBook ISBN 978-1-80078-101-6

Designed by Genevieve Webster
Edited by Alison Ritchie
Production by Neil Randles
Printed in China

a Shelter for Sadness

ANNE BOOTH & DAVID LITCHFIELD

templar
books

Sadness has come to live with me
and I am building it a shelter.

I am building a shelter for my Sadness
and welcoming it inside.

I am giving it a space
for it to sit

or lie down.

To curl up very,
very small,

or be as **big** as it can be.

To run around

or stand still.

To be **very,** **very noisy,**

or very, very quiet.

Or anything in between.

In this shelter for Sadness it can turn to the wall

or look out through the window, in the middle of the night . . .

or in the day.

The windows will open to let sounds in,

or close to keep them out.

The shelter I will build
for my Sadness
will have light from the sun
or from the moon and stars.

But the windows will have curtains
that Sadness can draw when it wants to.
And there will be candles or lamps
if Sadness needs them.

Lots and lots of light . . .

or no light at all.

Sadness can sit in darkness if it wants to.

Whatever it feels like.

Because this is the shelter for my Sadness,

and it has a right to be there.

And I will make my shelter strong, so that in winter

Sadness will have a safe shelter against the storms.

But I will give it a little garden too,
so that in spring, birds will come and build their nests
and green shoots will peek through the dark earth.

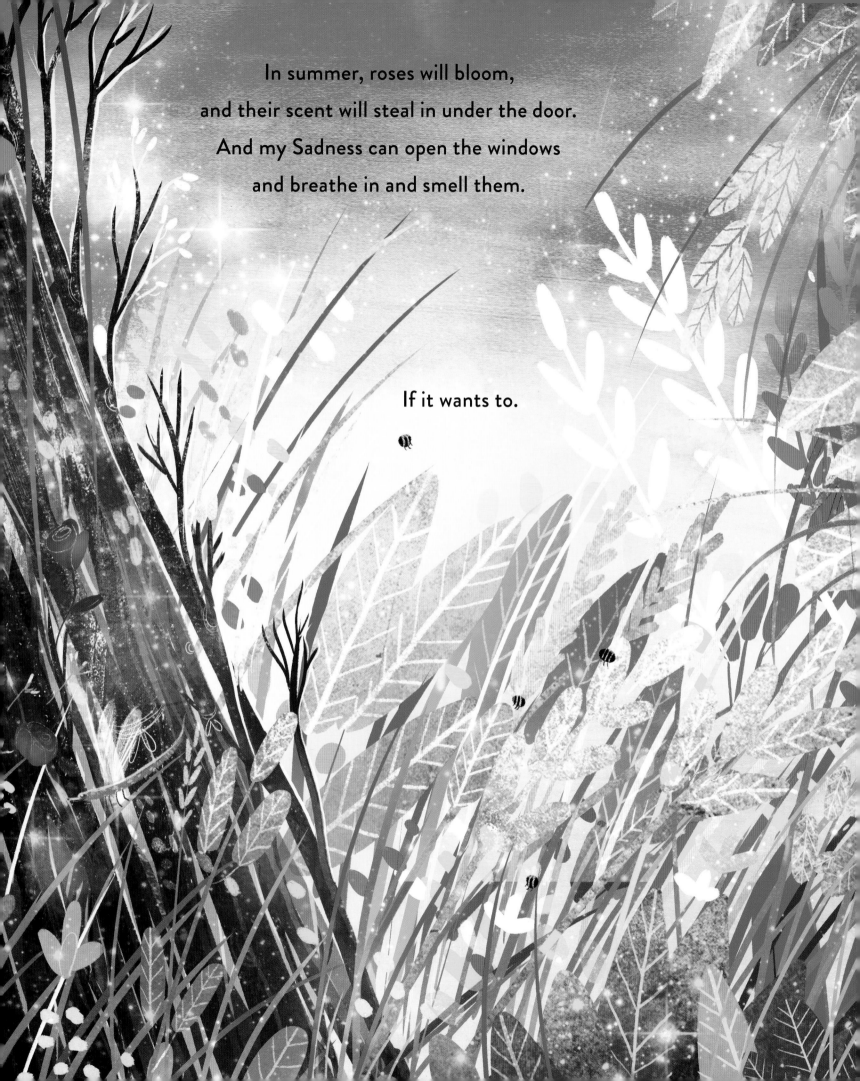

In summer, roses will bloom,
and their scent will steal in under the door.
And my Sadness can open the windows
and breathe in and smell them.

If it wants to.

In autumn it can look out at the trees,
and cry when the leaves turn red and orange
and fall to the ground.

Or it can go out and walk through the leaves
and hear the sounds they make.

It can build bonfires and dance around them,

or sit quietly and watch the flames.

Anything it needs to.

Sometimes I will visit my Sadness

in its shelter every day.

Every hour if needed.

Sometimes we will run

into each other's arms and hug and cry,

and talk . . .

and sometimes just sit next to each other

saying nothing.

Sometimes I will be too busy to visit Sadness for a while.

But that is okay too.

I have built a good shelter for my Sadness

and it is safe inside, and nobody will hurt it.

I can visit it whenever I need to.
Whenever it calls to me.

And, whenever Sadness wants,
it can come out of its shelter
and hold my hand.

And we will look out at the world

and discover how beautiful it is.

Together.